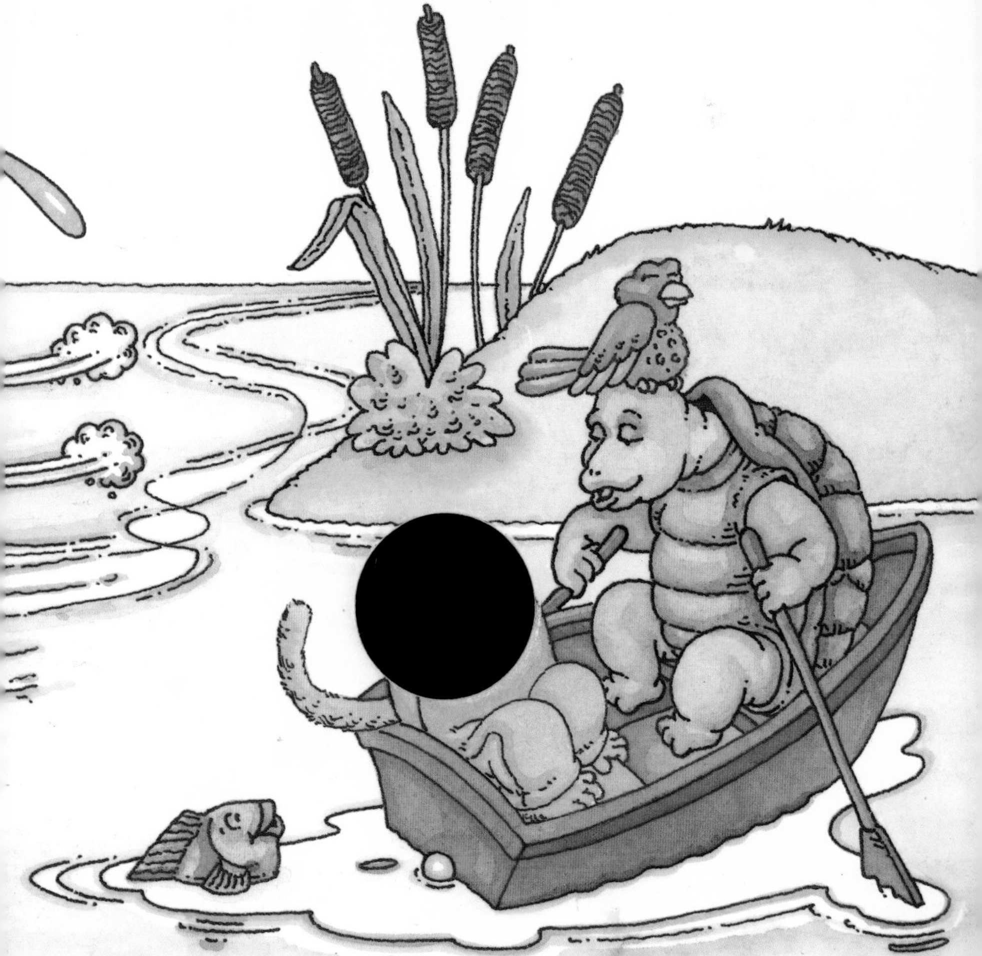

slow

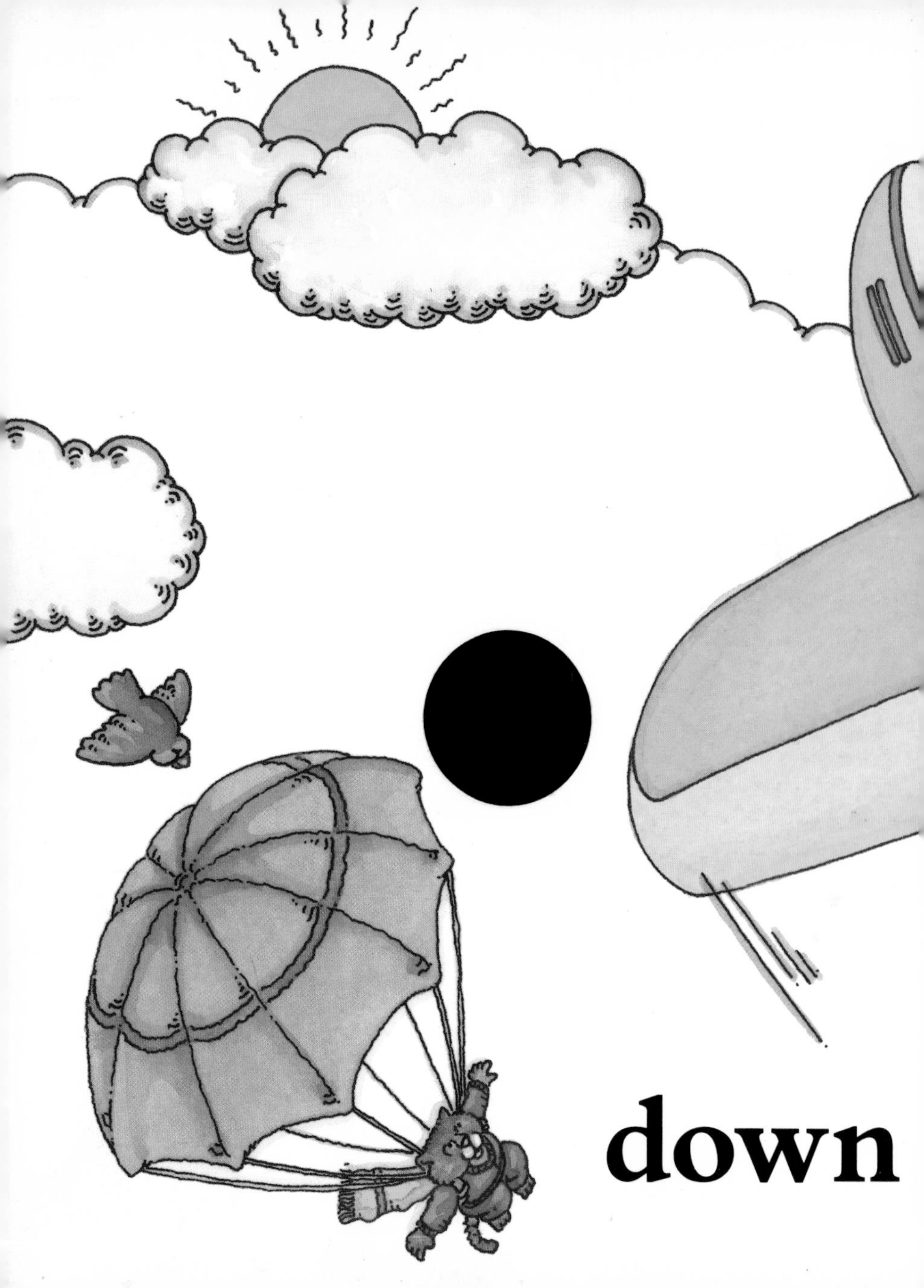

down

up

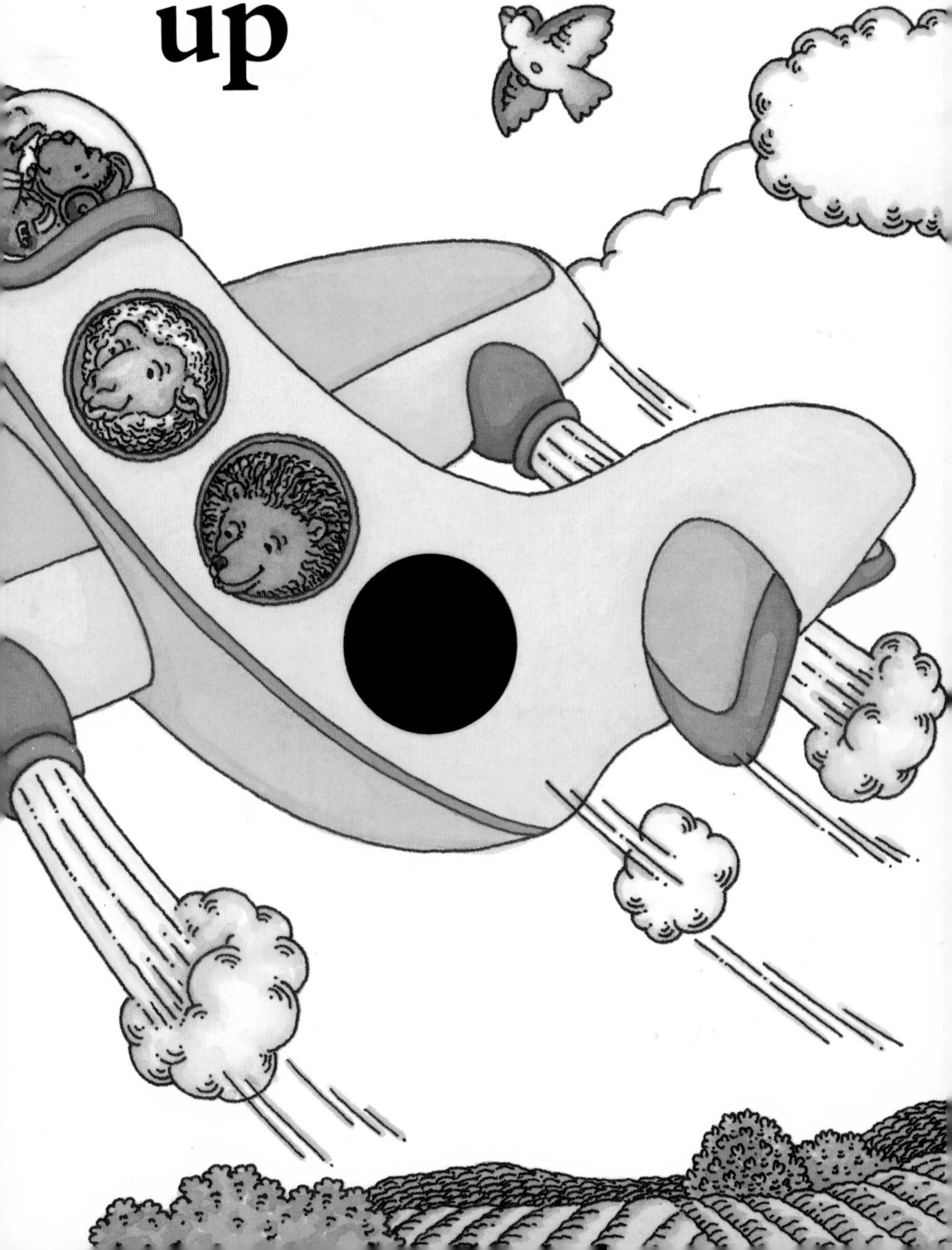

over

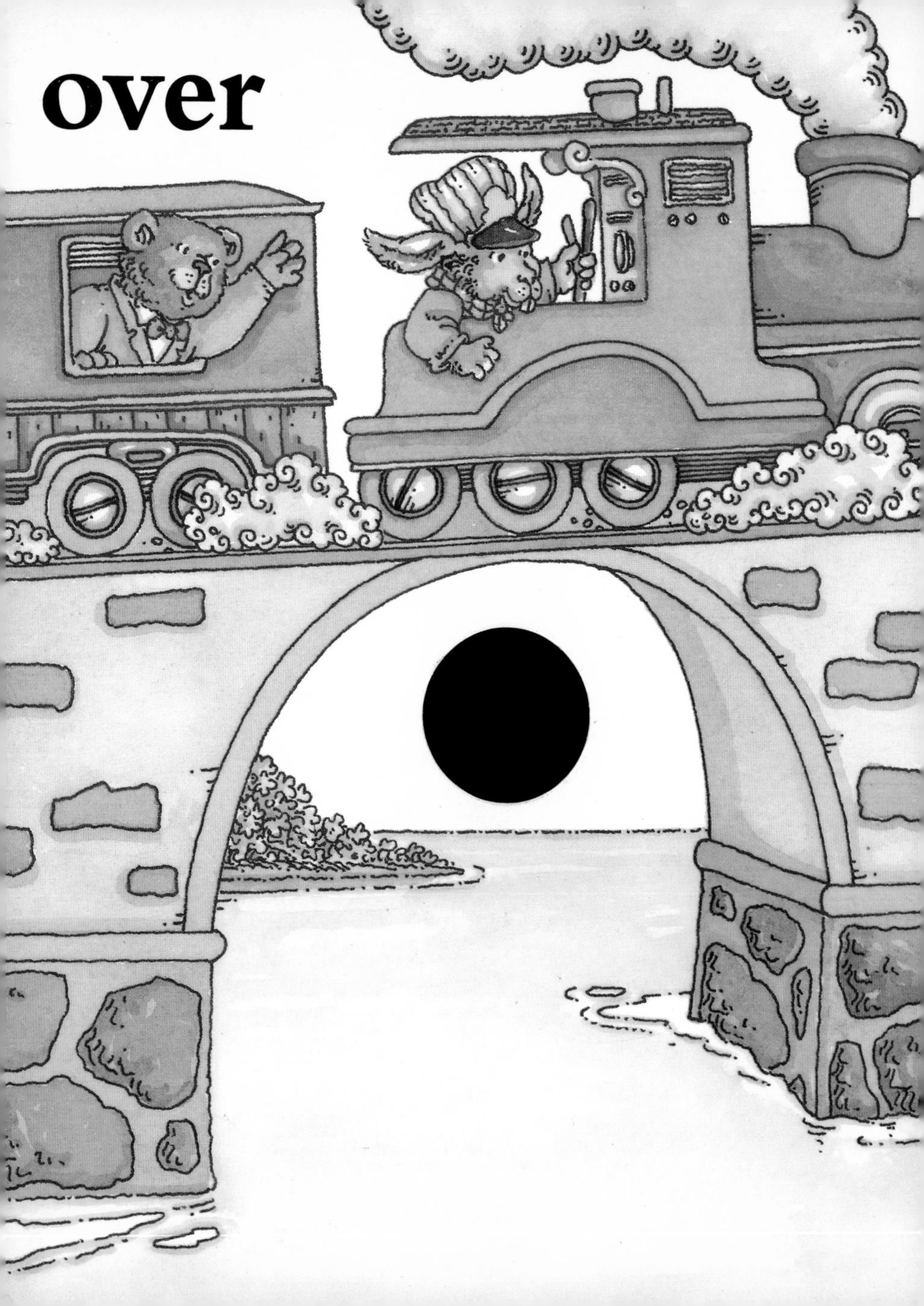

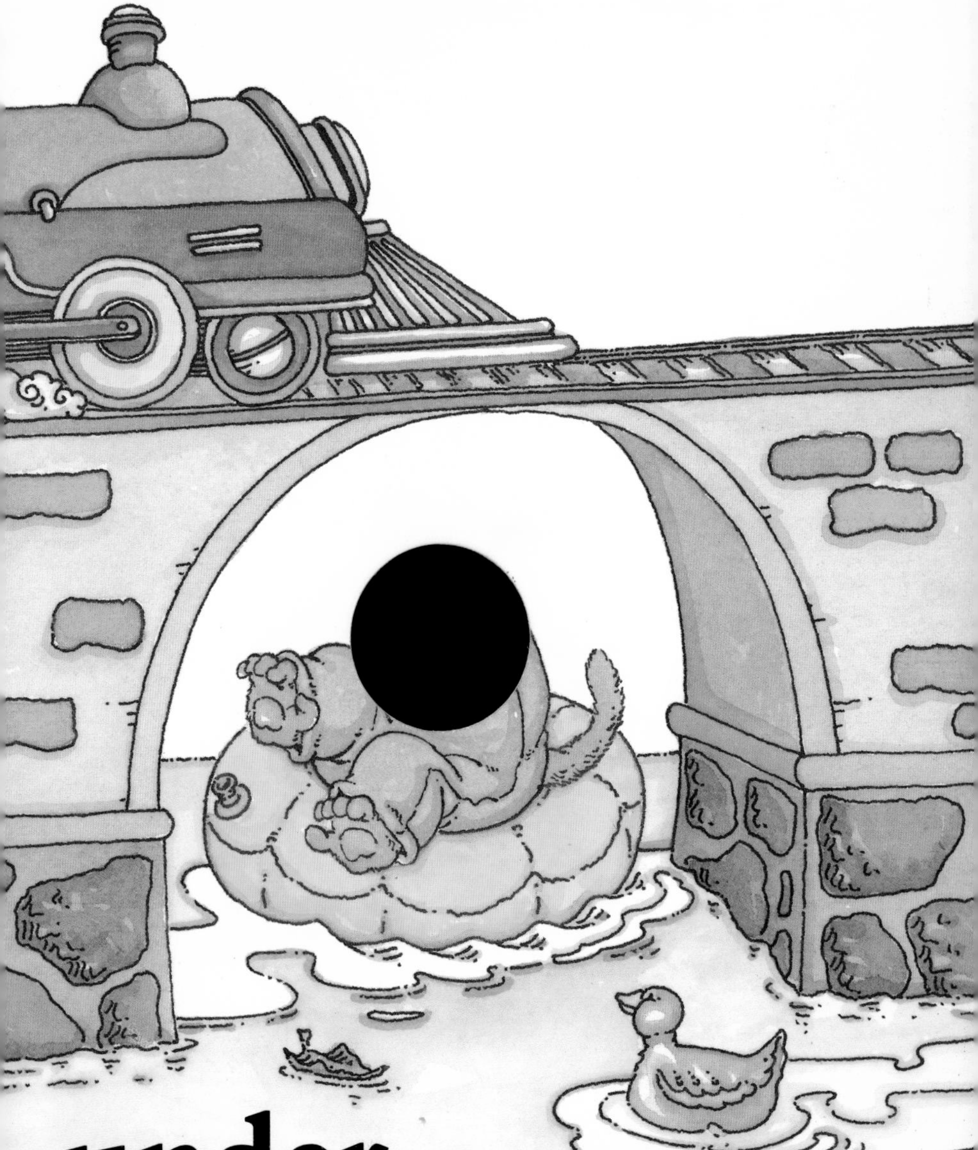

under

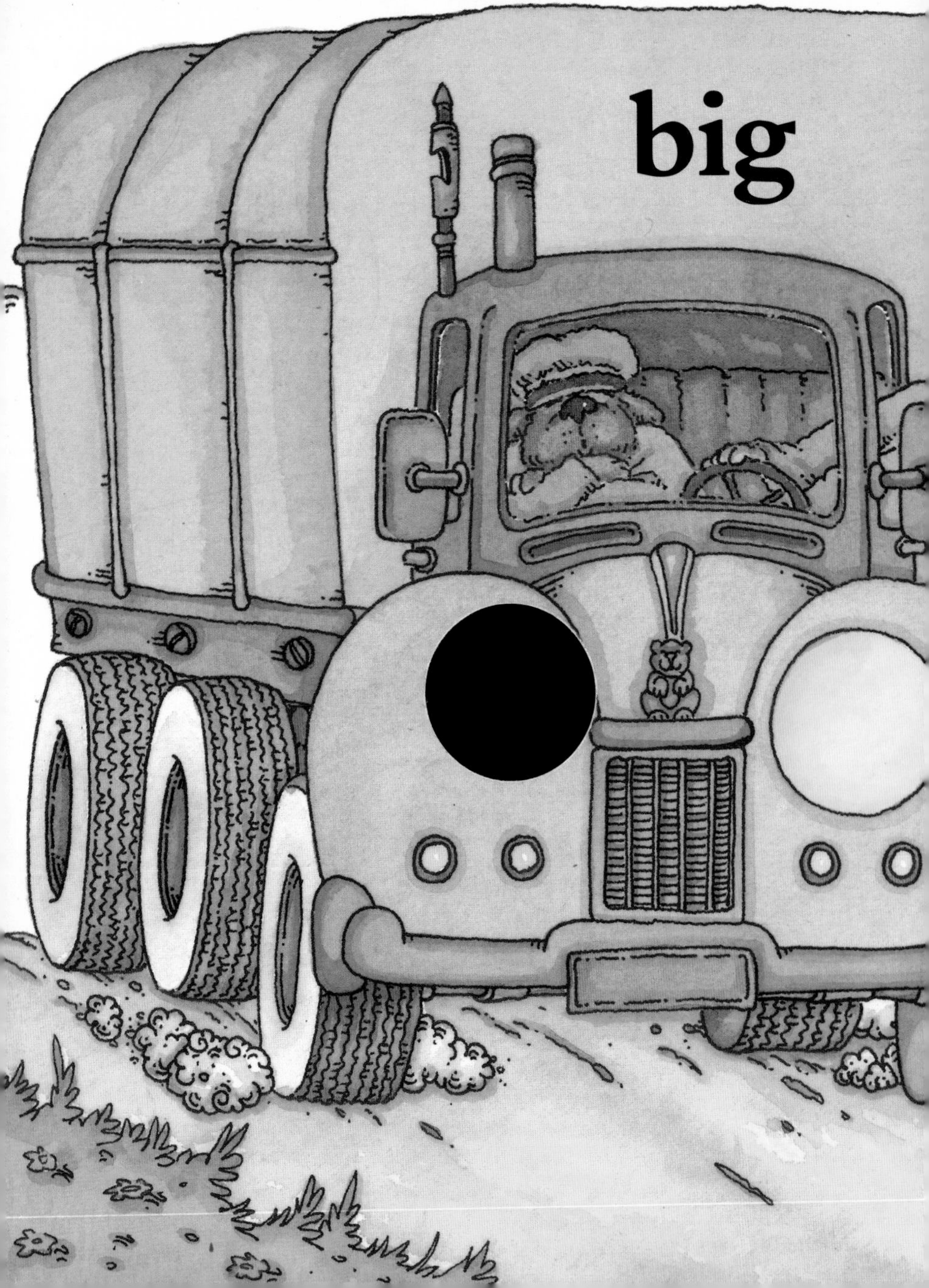

big

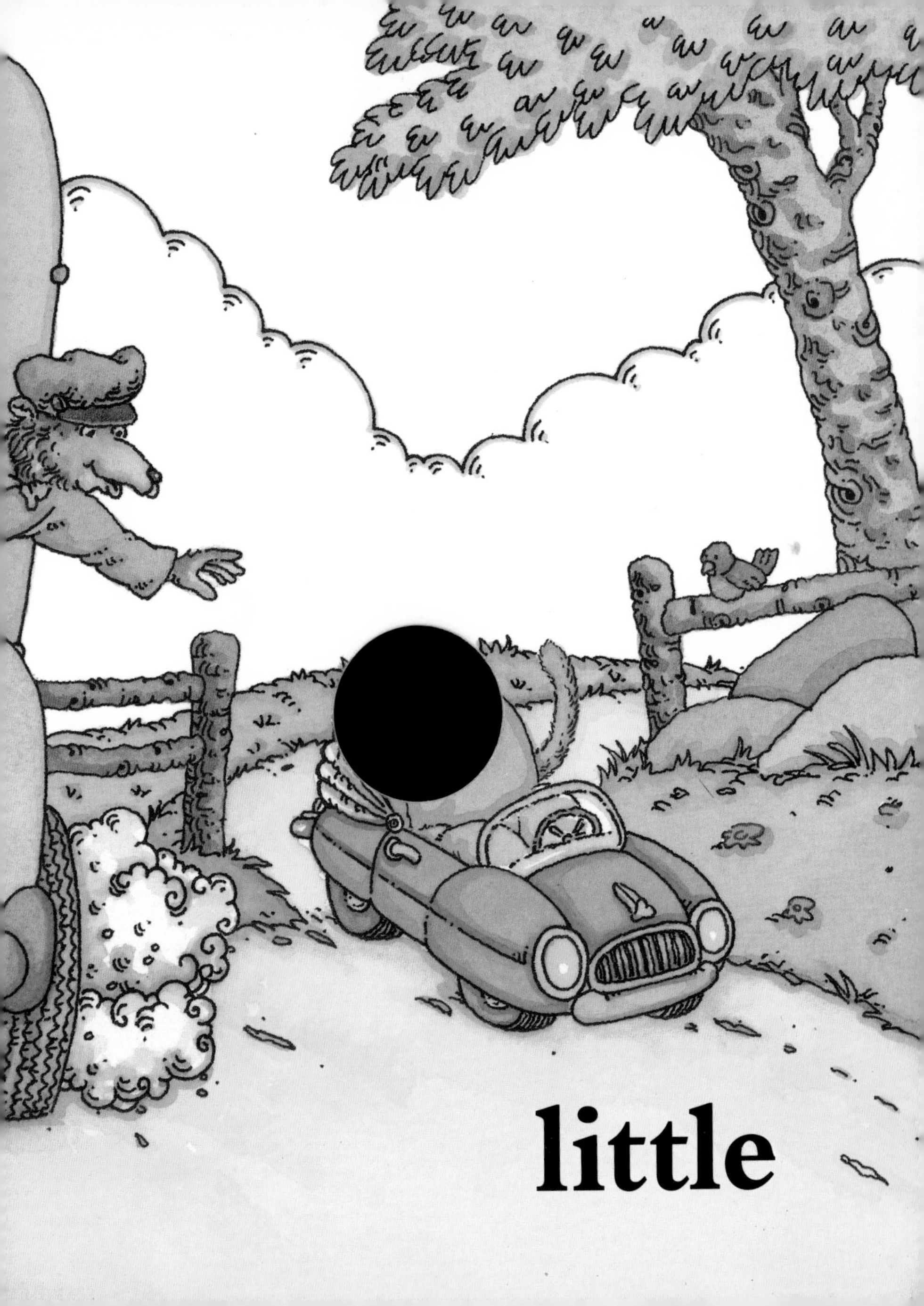

little

hot

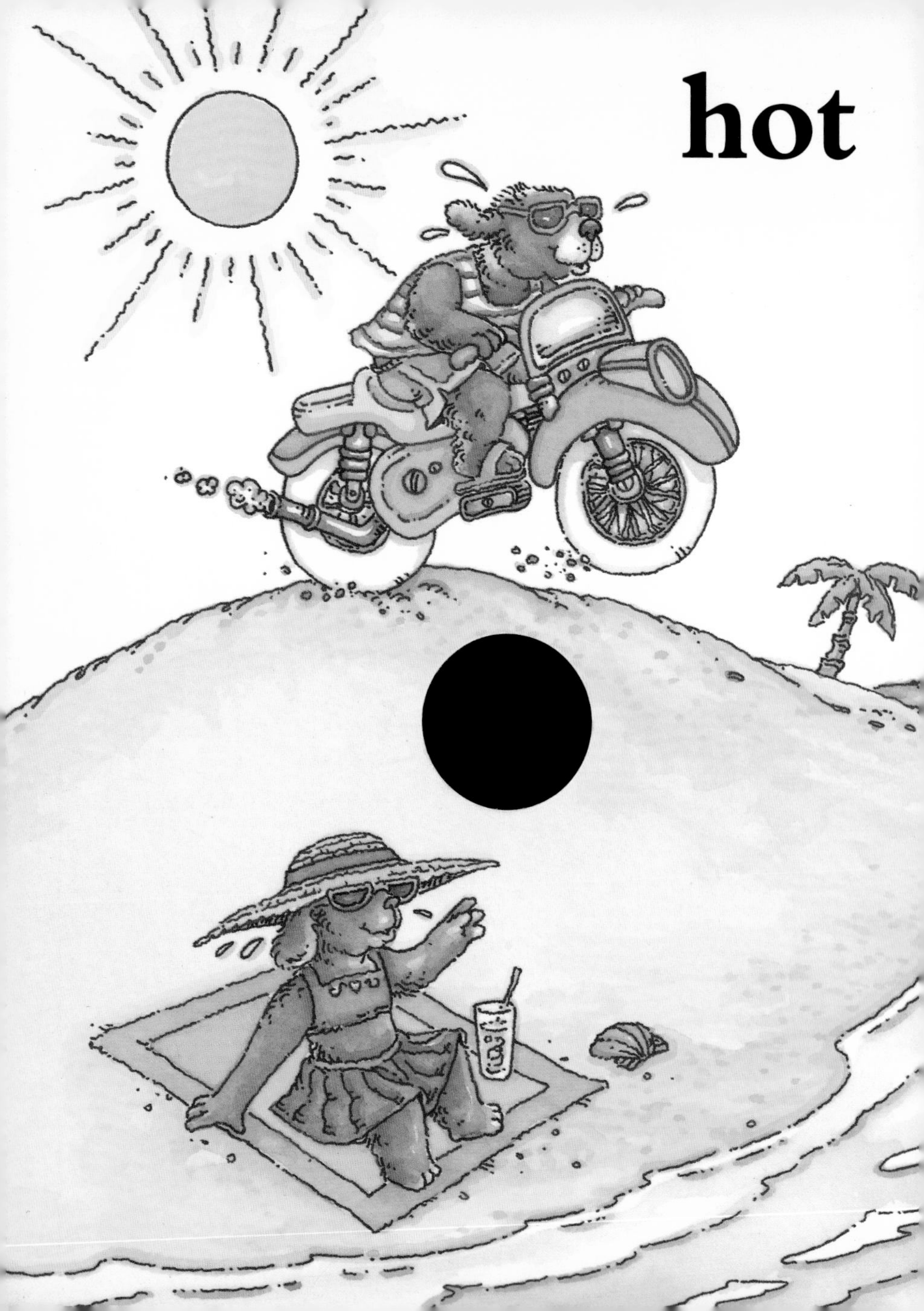

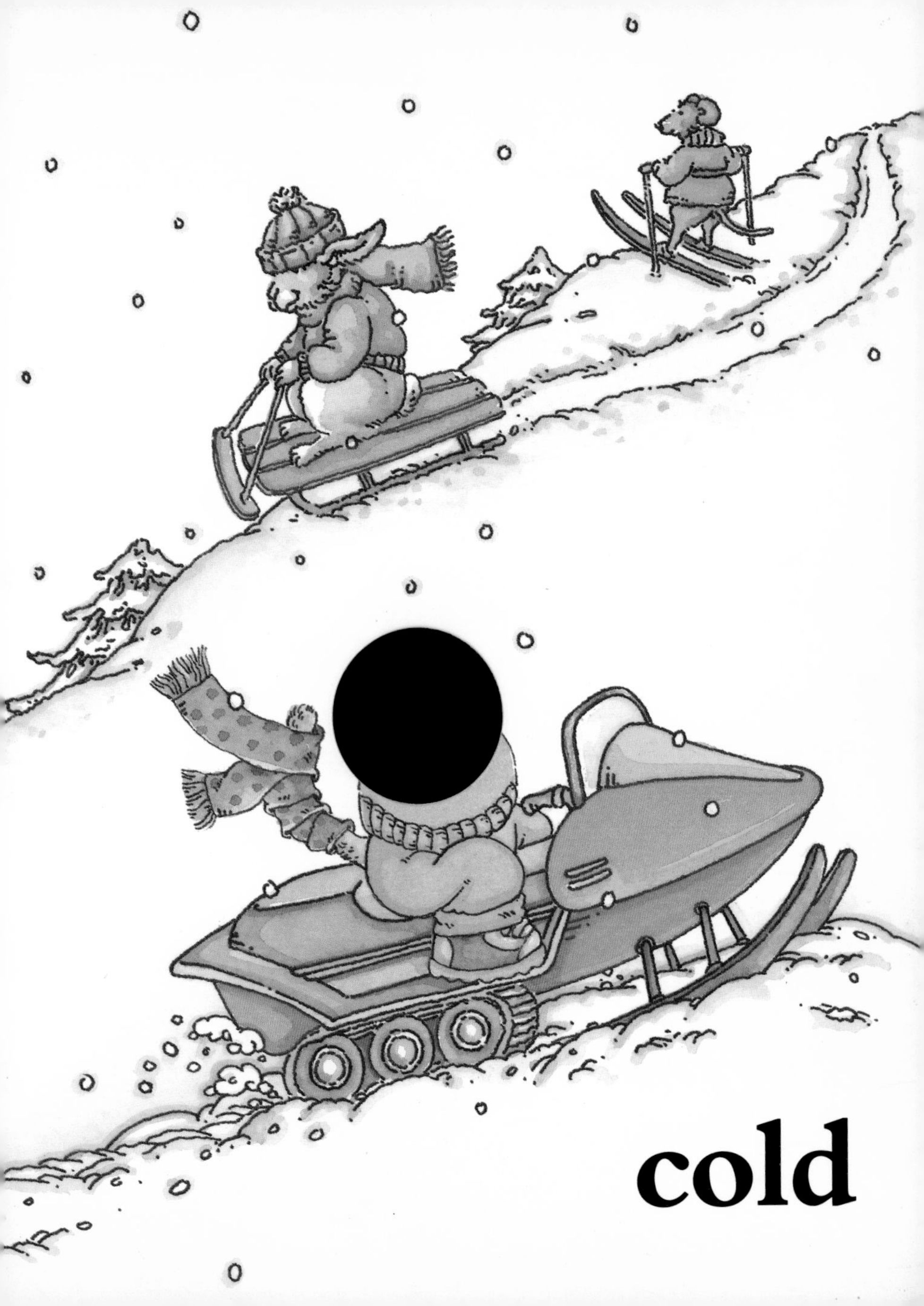

cold

top

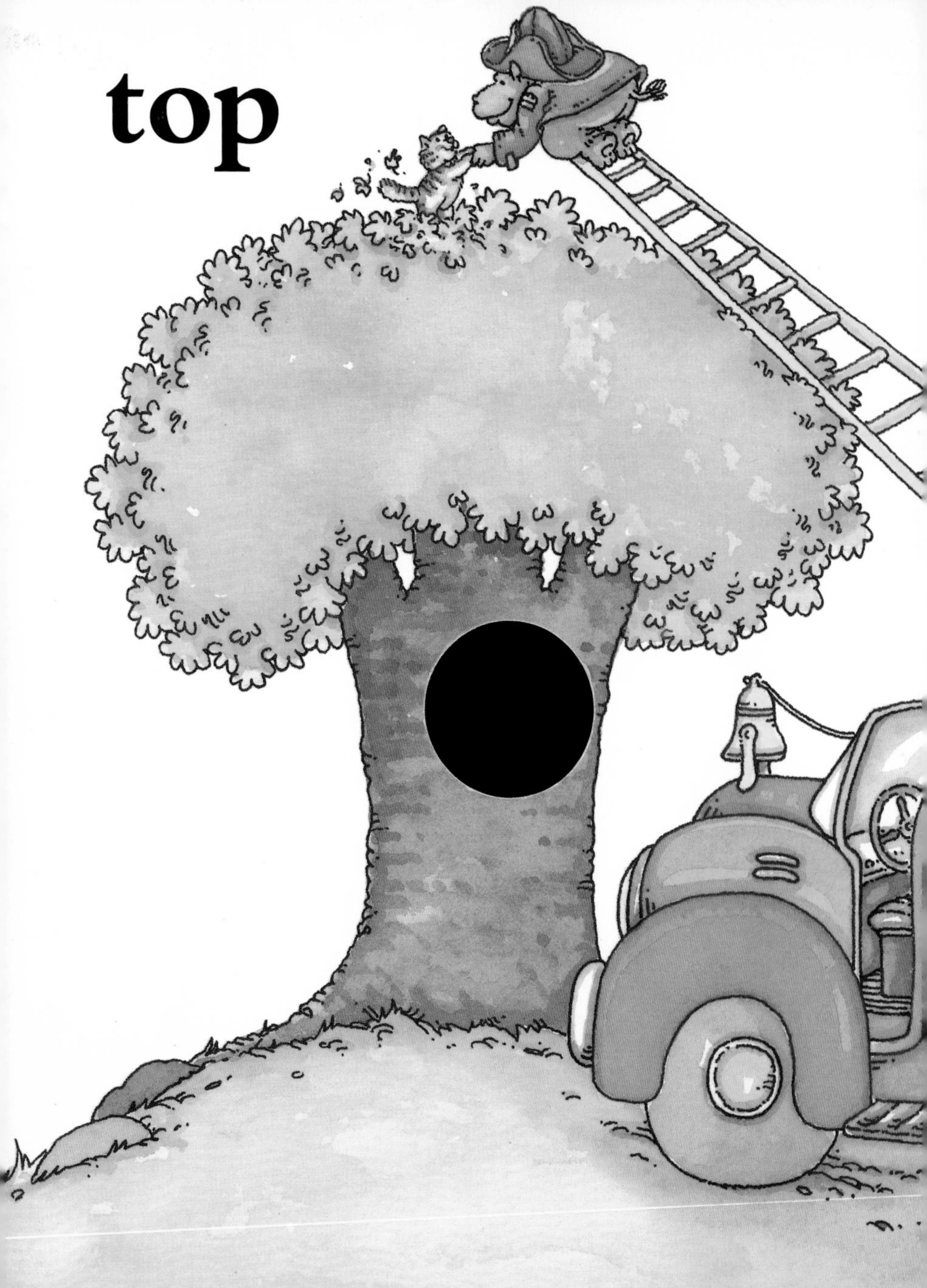

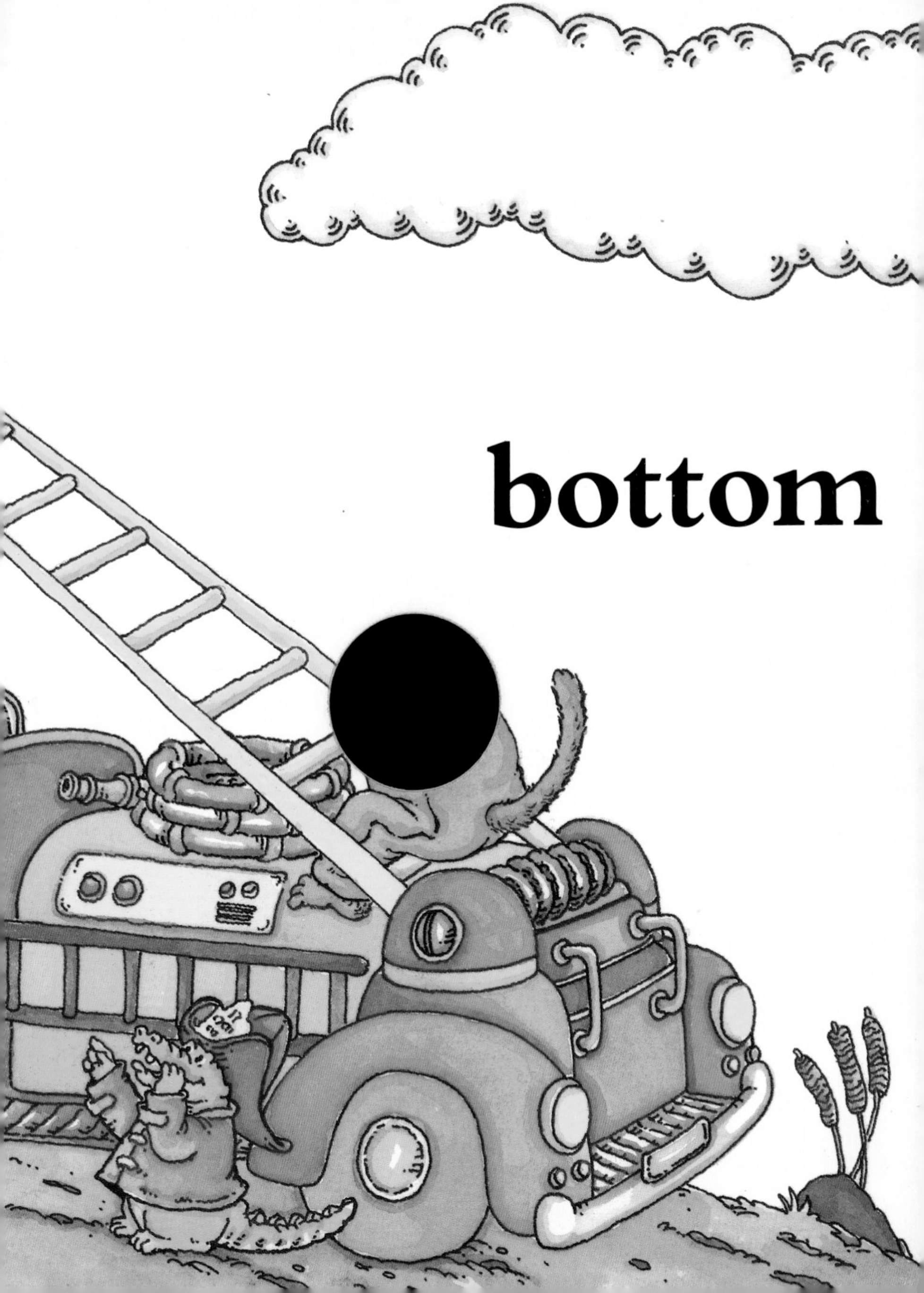

bottom

day

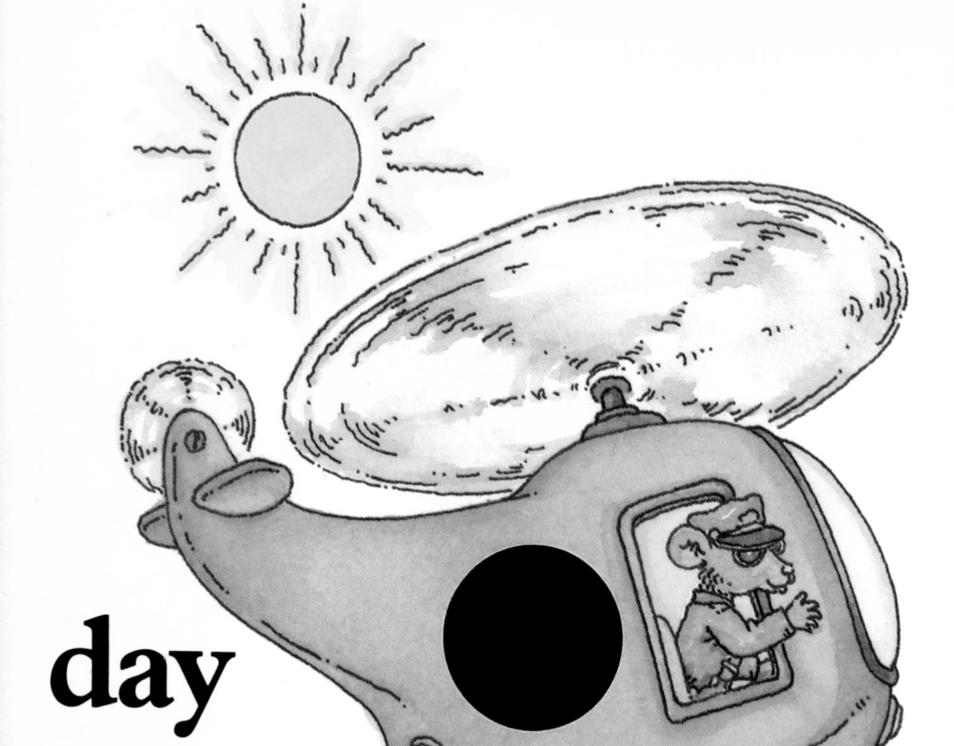

night

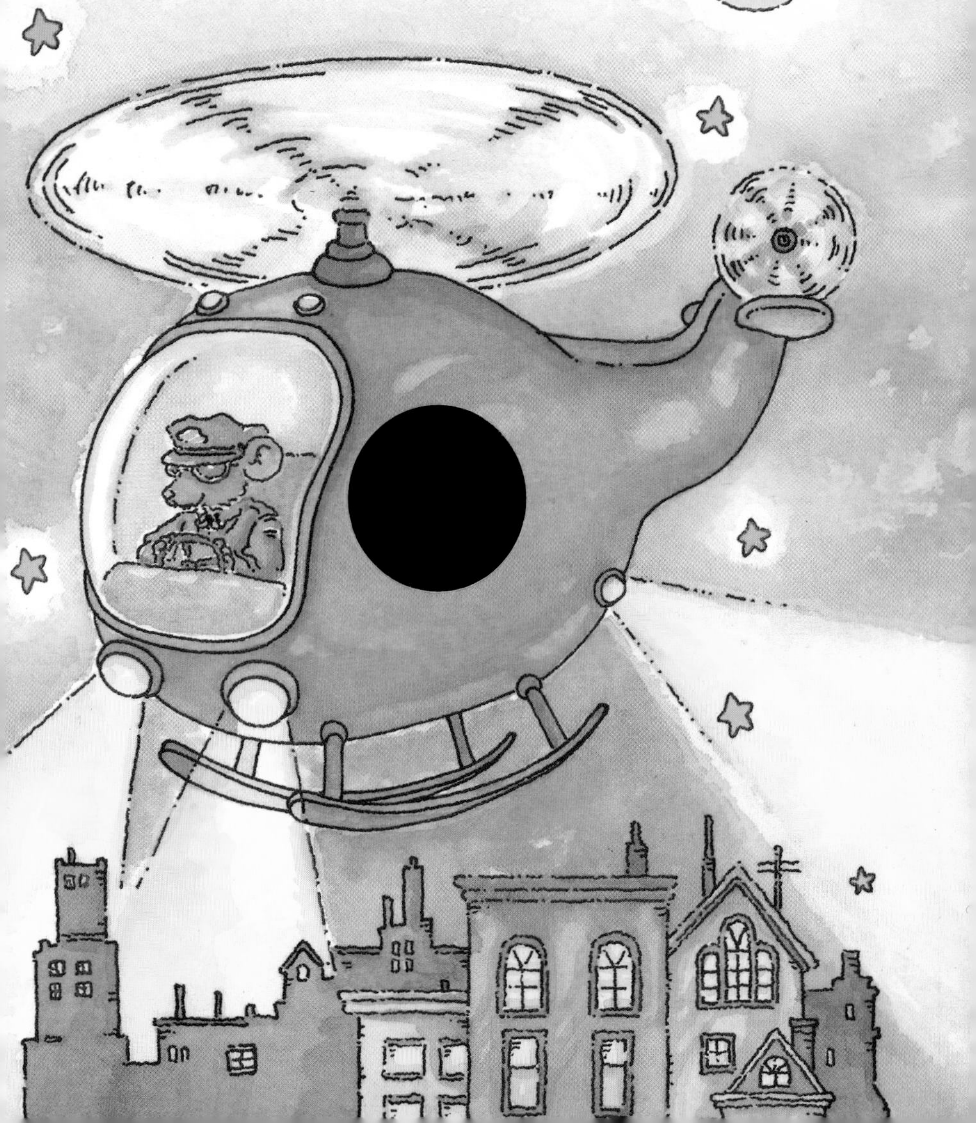

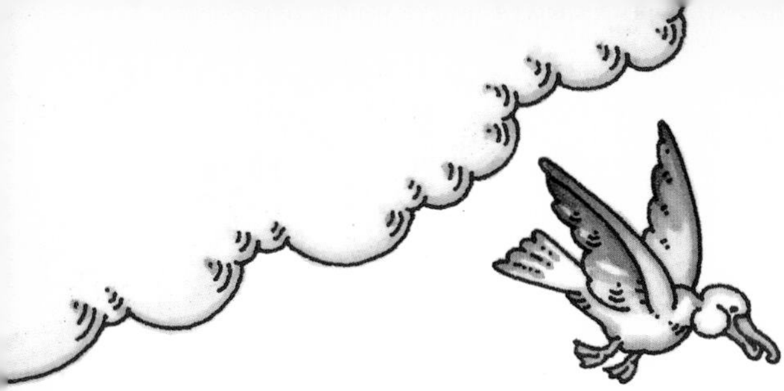

short

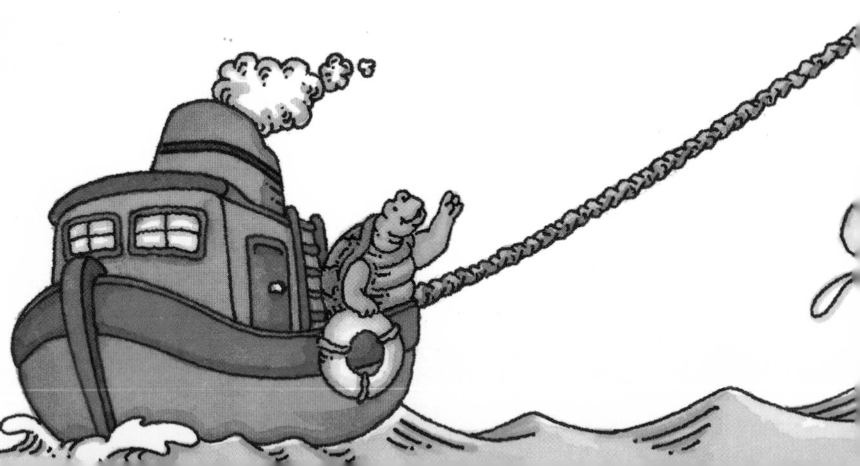

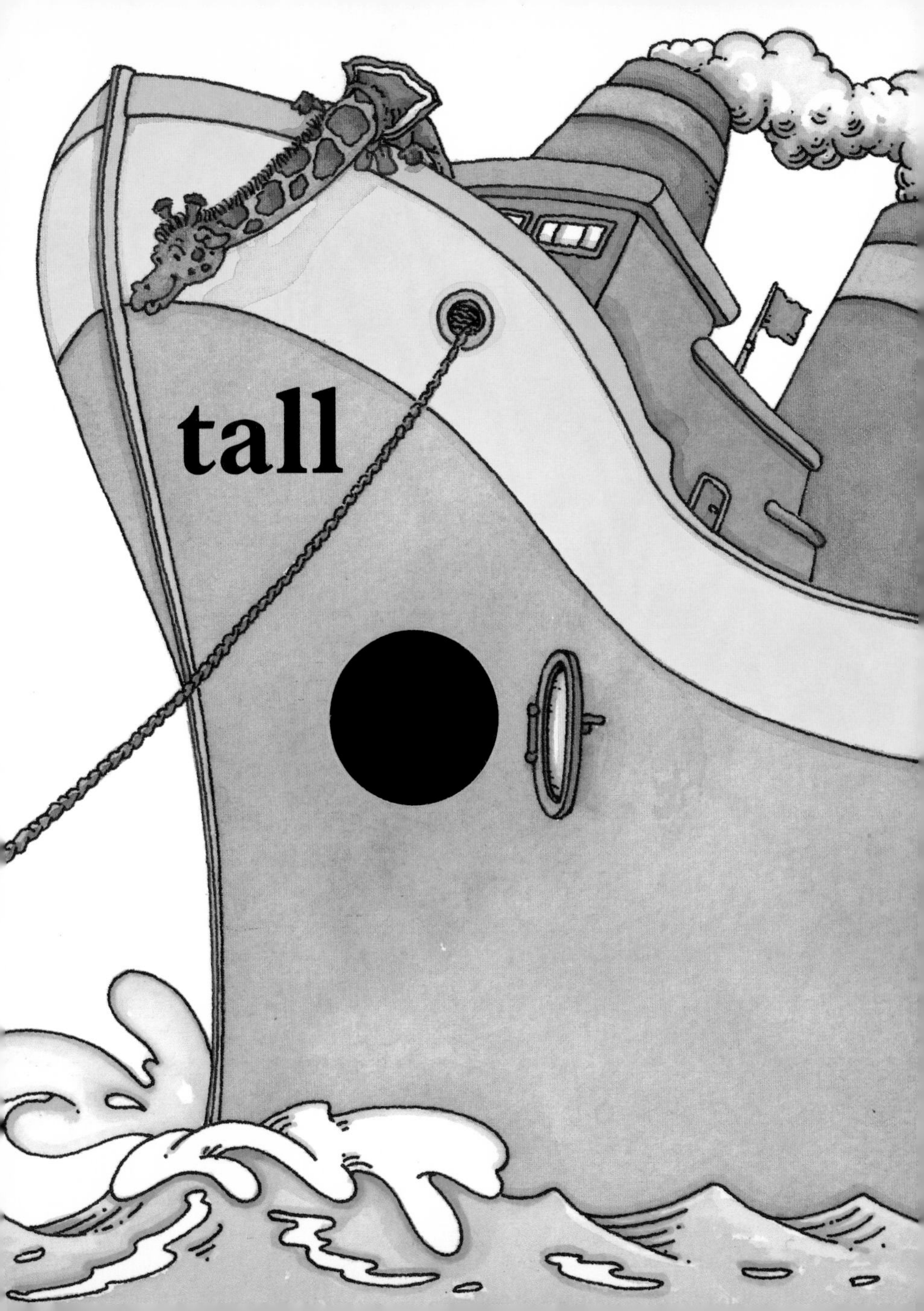

tall

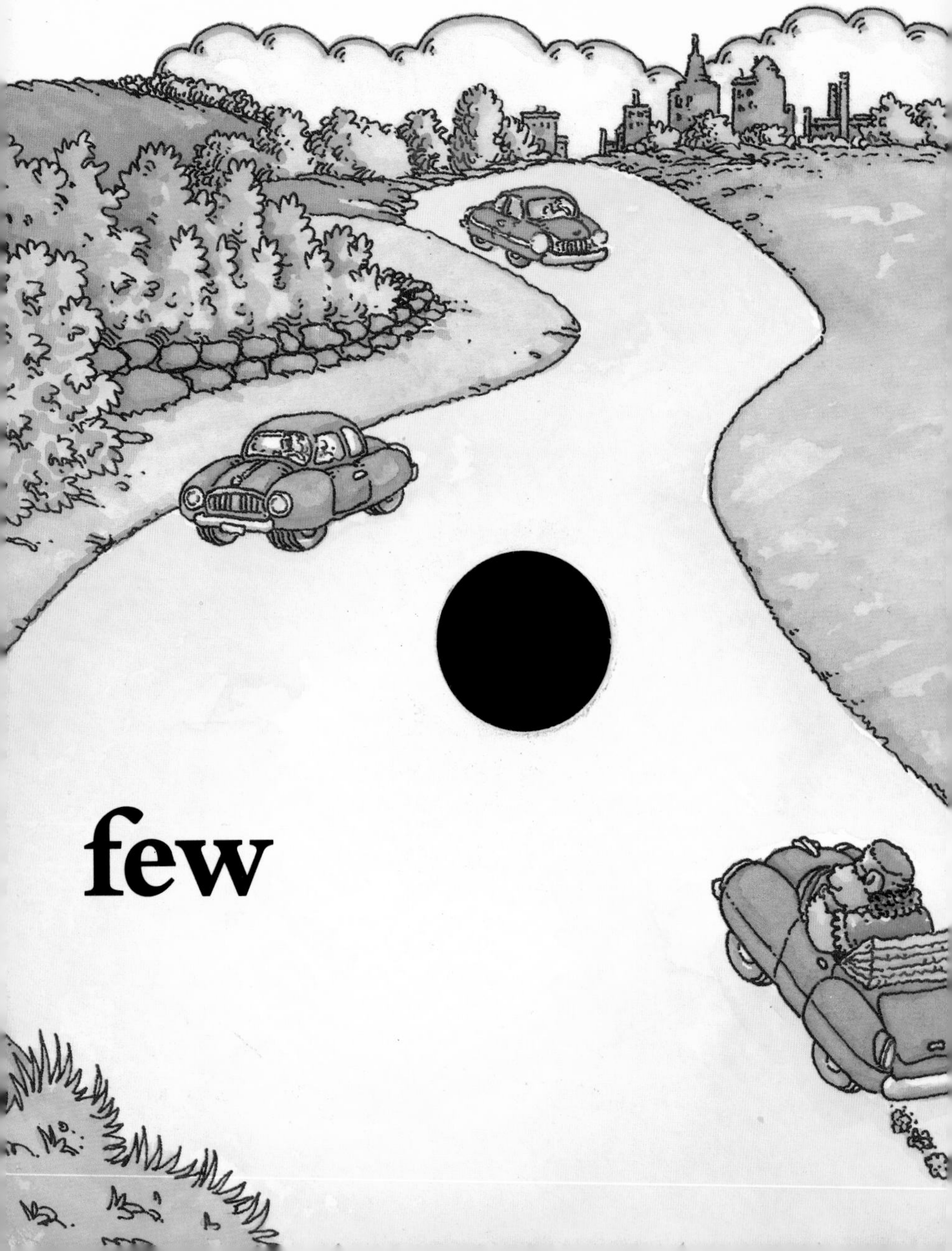

few

many

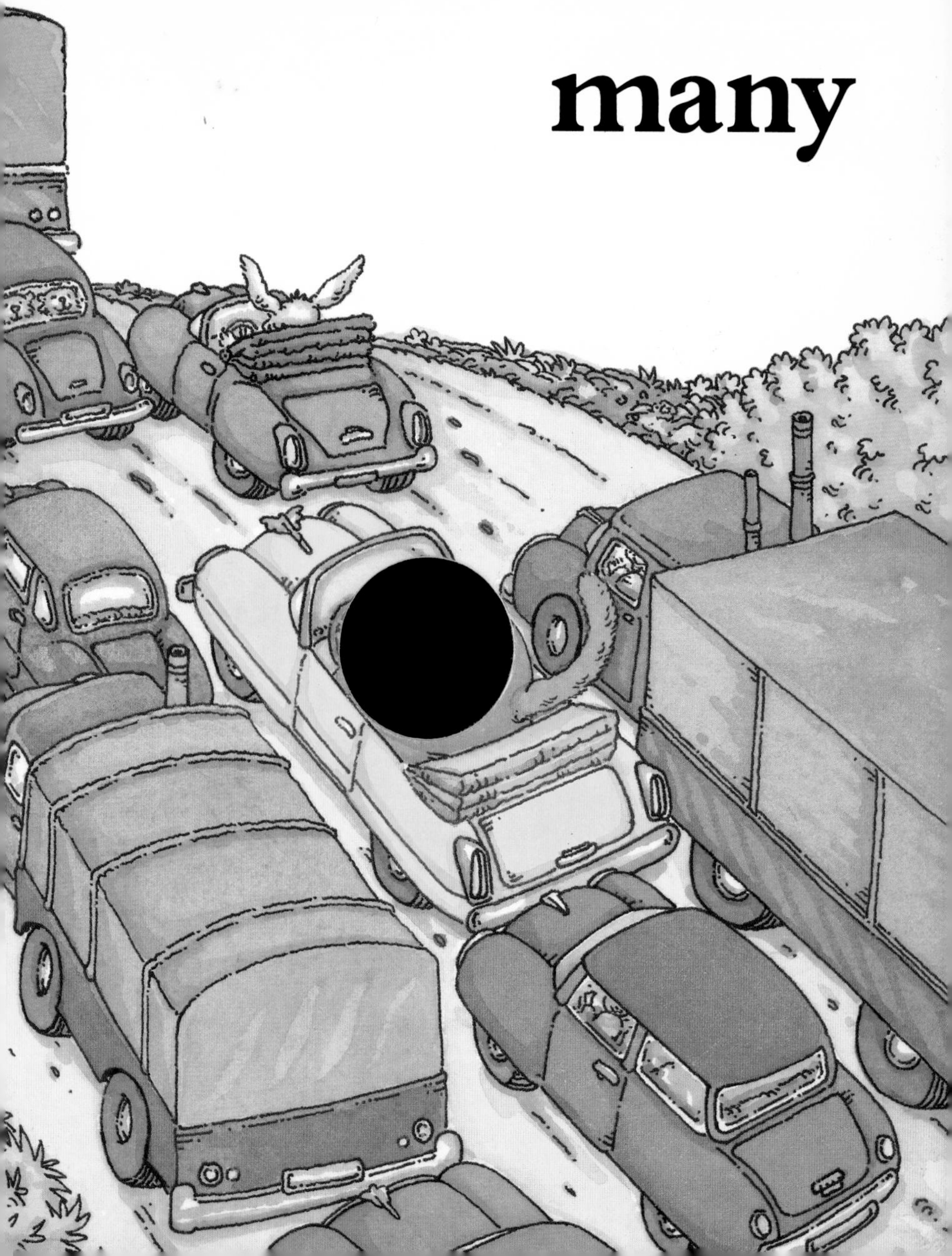

out

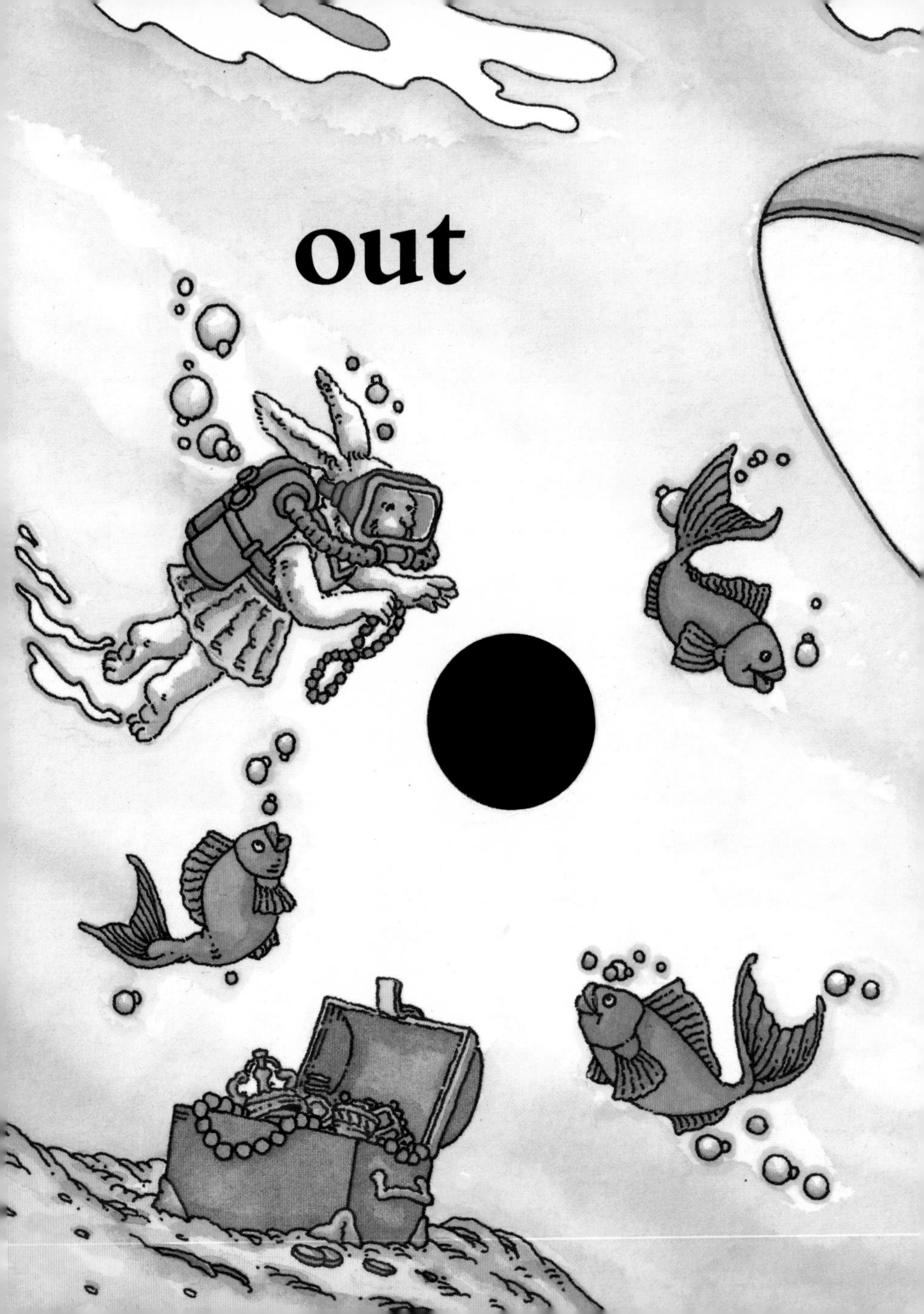

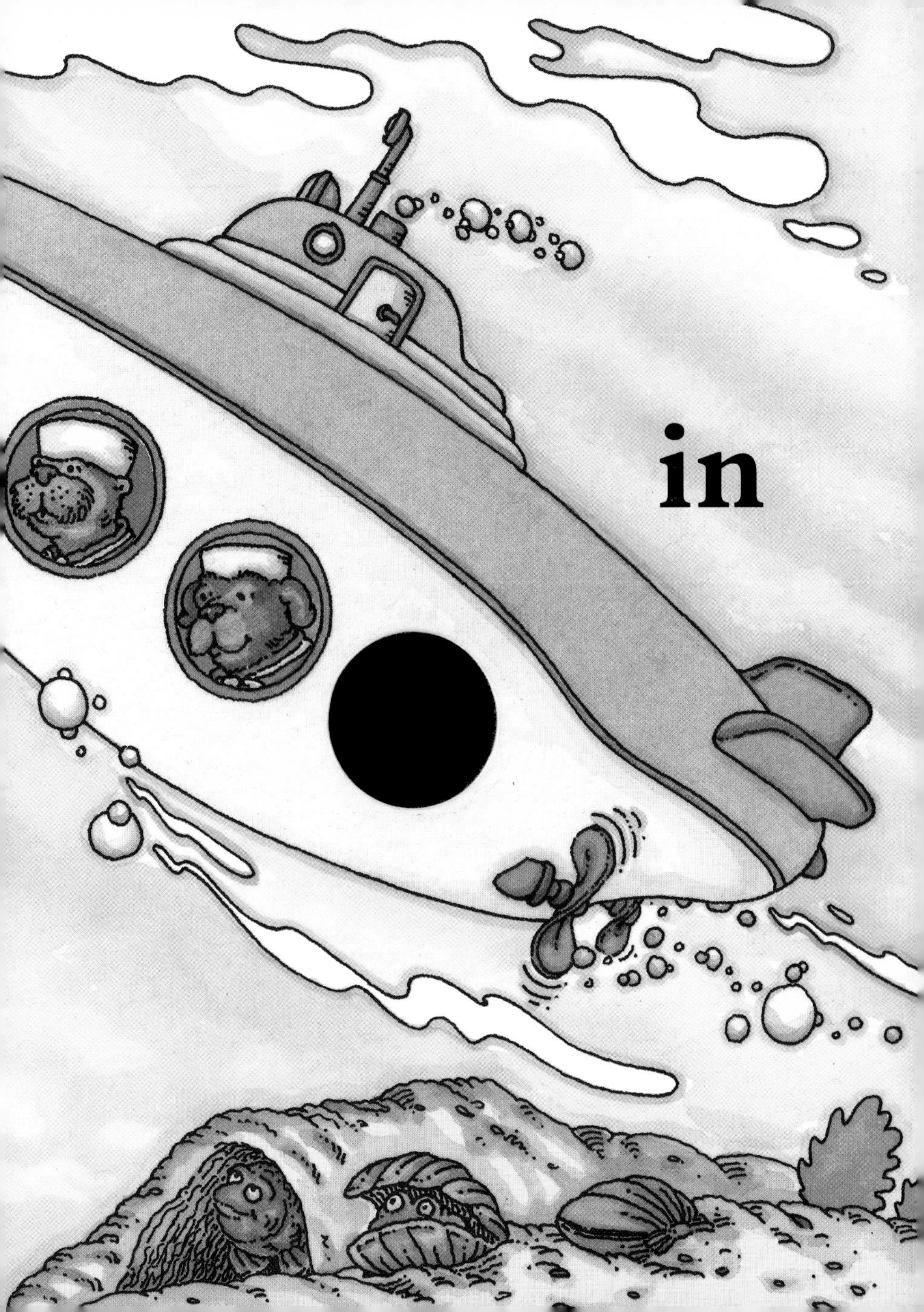

in

closed

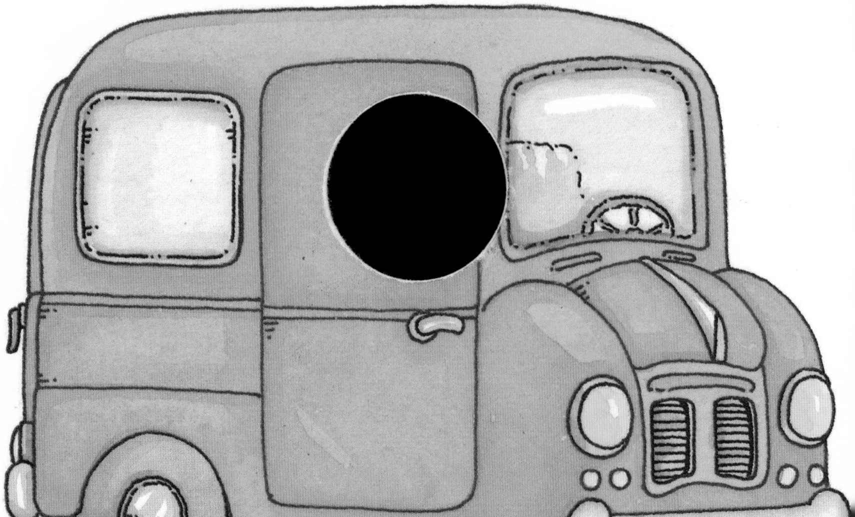